COWBOYS' INNOCENT AGE GAP

First Time Milking Story

Leandra Camilli

CONTENTS

CHAPTER 1

"And here is where you're going to sleep," the woman said, looking cheerful and happy that I was here. But my attention was turned elsewhere. The huge, menacing cowboy riding on horseback across the grassy fields around the farm. He was shirtless, the shadows shifting and moving on his spine.

I was already wet and paying very little attention to the introduction the woman was giving me.

The man was hypnotizing me. Something about him screamed that he wasn't from these parts or even this country.

His muscles were powerful, perfect like they were sculpted. On his face, on his chin, a hint of a beard that was still to be made. Sweat drops swirled down to his chin, pooling there and then breaking off every time he swung the rope.

He tied the loop again and hurled it across the field, catching the other horse that was trying to flee. He yanked the poor thing and it neighed, his bicep bulging and his abs growing tense and firm. I imagined myself sliding my hand over them, and then gliding it down to where his cock was.

Innocent? I was. A little. I hadn't had sex yet, after all.

Something made a snapping sound in front of me, and I snapped my head to it. I blinked twice and wasn't surprised when I found out that it was the guide, her brows furrowed.

"Are you even listening to me?" She asked, putting her hands on her waist.

"Yes, I am. I'm sorry. It's just that something caught my attention."

She softened up her expression, taking her hands off her waist and lowering her shoulders. Shaking her head, she joked, "I know he's handsome and a jaw-dropper, but if you disappoint him, he won't have any trouble kicking you out."

"I know," I murmured, my eyes paying attention to her for the next few minutes or so. She entered the barn and I went there with her.

The cowboy had already gotten off the back of the horse and was now by the side of the barn, filling a bucket with water.

He swiped his forearm across his forehead, his muscles flexing under the hot sunlight. I was getting so wet that my legs were already feeling wet. I thought that the tampon and my pair of panties were enough to contain my leak. Fuck. Things were getting out of hand.

By my side was a crack and through it, I could peek at the cowboy. He had the side of his body turned toward me and was crouching on the soil. He turned off the faucet and the water stopped gushing out of it. His hand looked big. From a distance, it was difficult to judge how big of a man he was, but now I was getting a better look at it and I could tell that if he were to enclose his hand around my neck, he'd made me feel even tinier than I was.

Even my friends called me short and petite. Before that mighty man, I'd look like a midget, and that would be a good thing. I could just imagine him engulfing me in his heavy body, and then burying his cock into my needy pussy…

And then, he snapped his eyes up. Like he'd already known, this whole time, that I was peeking at him through the hole in the wall. His eyes were intense, determined, and focused on me.

I felt that I was frozen in place more than I already was. He was still holding the bucket in his hand – just one of them – like the weight of it filled with the water didn't mean anything to him.

His stare was telling me a million things, and none of them were bad. He had plans for me. I was sure of that.

Another snapping sound in front of me, and I was taken back to reality. The cowboy stood up, hands holding the bucket, and then walked away toward where he left his horse. I glanced him over from bottom to top, and then returned my attention to the guide.

She sighed, sitting on a log put on the floor.

"You know, I really thought that you were going to turn differently than the others."

"Than the others?" I quizzed, curious about what she was referring to.

"That's the way he is. Once he has his eyes on you, there's no turning back. You are his woman now."

I blinked twice, not understanding what she was talking about.

Seeing that, the guide sighed. "You are not the first woman who applied to work here, and they all ended up getting changed. They all chose to go through the transformation."

"What transformation? What are you talking about?" I asked, taking a step toward her.

The guide stood up. She narrowed her eyebrows as she took a step toward me.

"There's no point in explaining it. You are going to meet up with him tonight, right?"

I took a step backward, whirling around and then running out of the barn. When I was crossing the door, I stumbled on something heavy and warm. I fell on my ass and looked up, finding another cowboy in front of me.

He was glaring down at me, showing me that he didn't care about me one bit. He was just as strong and imposing as the other cowboy, and he could be just one person. He had to be the other owner of the farm, and he was also shirtless.

Glancing down, I couldn't help but realize that he was hard, his cock straining against his pants. Pulling up the corner of his lips, he smiled without showing his teeth.

He held out a hand and I took it, feeling how strong and big it was. He pulled me up and I lost my balance, falling into his arms. He held me against his body and I could feel again how warm it was. It was like the man was the sun itself.

"Hey, sweetheart. I know this is your first day on the job, but there's no need to be like this. Take things easy." He turned his eyes so that he was peeking over my shoulders, his hand roaming over my spine. "I'm going to take things from here."

And I knew that, from then on, I wasn't going to be seeing the guide again.

CHAPTER 2

He was taking me through a path just behind the farm-house, being a couple of feet in front of me. I was trying to keep up with him, but it was difficult. His legs were very long and he walked with determination, his posture nothing short of perfect.

I accelerated so that I was by his side when he put one of his hands against my shoulders all of a sudden, pushing me up against the wall. I glanced up, first noticing his chest and then his lips. They were perfect. Not too big and not too thin, either.

"I know about the way you were looking at Walter, and I don't like that," he growled, his hands massaging my shoulders.

I knew who he was talking about, but I was still going to pretend I didn't.

"What?" I asked and he tsked.

"Don't play coy with me." I searched his eyes and I knew he was thinking the same thing I was. He moved his hand behind my neck, entangled his fingers in my hair, and then pulled my head up so that I was crashing my lips against his.

I supposed I should be saying that he was crushing my lips.

He was relentless, brushing his fingers over the back of my head as his lips continued to stroke my mouth. He was warm – warmer than the air around him. His hold was strong and determined and even if I was trying to push him away from me, I wouldn't be able to do that.

He was suffocating me and it felt good. I wrapped my arms around his neck and gave myself to him. He smirked even though we were still smooching each other, one of his hands moving over my back and cupping my right asscheek.

"Gosh, you are irresistible," he murmured into my mouth as he kissed me one more time with his eyes closed.

But it was just a peck. Moments later, he stopped the kiss and checked me out from top to bottom. His eyes were full of lust and how much he wanted me.

"Should we take this somewhere more private? How about my colleague's room?" He proposed, his voice low and sexy. I squirmed as I didn't know what he wanted my answer to be.

Even though it was clear he wanted to have sex with me, I had no idea if he was playing me right now. I knew what cowboys like him were like, after all.

He grabbed my arm, taking me away from there when he flew away from me all of a sudden. His body slid over the grass, eyes shooting up as he tried to figure out what just happened. I snapped my head where that came from and I wasn't surprised when I realized that it was Otis who had done that.

He was huffing, beads of sweat pooling on his forehead. His fist was still lifted and then he lowered it, eyes looking red and angry. I didn't know what was going on in his mind, but it couldn't be anything good.

"You're not taking her away from me," he growled, leaping toward Walter, who was just jumping back up. I knew what was happening, and I didn't know if it was a good thing. They were both fighting over me.

They were both fighting over me when they could have me at the same time.

Walter leaped at Otis, landing a solid and heavy punch on his gut. One punch after the other, a kick that didn't hit the right place, and a pull of the hair, and then they were both panting and tired.

Sweat pooling on their foreheads, they looked even more frightening and handsome than usual. To say that I was wet right now would be an understatement.

And I was also flattered that they both thought I was worth it. I couldn't wrap my head around the fact that, on my first day on the job, both of my employers were fighting for ownership of me.

I couldn't help but imagine myself riding on both of their dicks over and over, and they hurting me until they were cumming inside my snatch.

I almost lost my consciousness when I realized that there was a shadow behind the water tank of the farm. It moved and the person who was there showed up, sighing as she realized that what was happening was pointless.

"You know, this fight shouldn't even be happening. Isn't it true that you both used to share your recruits? I'm sure she will become a very fertile hucow as well, but you can both have her," she lamented, shaking her head and then turning around and trudging away.

"What?" I squeaked, surprised more than anything that she read my mind and seemed to set the cowboys straight. They fixed their postures, looking less like they were going to go at it again, and then Walter strode over to stand in front of me.

He grabbed my hand and, together with Otis, took me to the other barn in the farmhouse – the one that I wasn't allowed to go into. It looked like things were changing here, and for the better.

I wouldn't have been able to live in this place and fight against my curiosity for long without getting in here and finding out what they were keeping hidden there.

And I shouldn't be surprised that this was their dirty little secret. Hucows, one after the other, locked up in their pens as their eyes diverted to me. They mooed like they were approving of something, or someone. There were so many of them it was almost impossible to count.

Walter grabbed my left ass cheek and squeezed it. When I

peeked over my shoulder and at his eyes, I knew he had something life-changing to say to me.

"Looks like they approve of you."

CHAPTER 3

They did, and now it looked like something fundamental was going to change in my life. Locked up in the basement of the farmhouse, I couldn't help but feel like I'd been made for this. Licking my lips, I couldn't wait until the cowboys were walking into the room and then ravaging my mouth with their thick, long cocks.

The door creaked open and I knew that the moment I'd been waiting for was finally happening. I heard both of their footsteps walking over to me, making me feel a shiver running down my spine.

They weren't just going to turn me into one of the hucows. They were going to take my mouth's virginity, too.

"So, my pretty little princess, on a scale of 1 to 10, how much do you want this to happen?" Otis queried, putting his hand under my chin and lifting my head.

"Eleven. Eleven! I want you to fuck me until there's nothing left of the old me," I responded, my voice throaty and heavy.

I couldn't see his face in the darkness of the room, but I knew that he was smirking. He took his hand off my chin and I could hear his hands working as he removed his belt. Then, his pants fell to the floor and I could feel his body standing right in front of me.

I could also hear his hand stroking his dick, getting it hard and nice for me. He settled his hand behind my head and, with a shove, brought it down with force. I was forced to open my lips wide before I even realized what was happening.

Moments later, he was all the way inside my mouth and lodged in my throat. He was so big that he was already hurting my throat and mouth, and I couldn't even move my tongue over his dick the way I wanted to. I had no idea if I was pleasing the man, but there was also no denying he was already moaning.

His fingers dug into the skin of my head as he started to move it up and down, and then down and up, fucking my mouth. He was relentless, picking up speed soon after.

His balls were bouncing off against my chin and even though I was feeling a lot of pain, I was also feeling a lot of pleasure.

My body was resonating with what he was doing and I just wanted this to go on for as long as possible. I was on my knees and chained up to one of the walls of the basement. Chains rattled every time he shoved his shaft up against the upper side of my throat.

When I thought he was already getting his fill, he pumped up his pace and continued to destroy my mouth for what felt like an eternity. My body moving with the speed he was employing, I tried to keep up with him as my boobs bounced up and down.

My pussy was wetter than it had ever been, and I couldn't help but wait with impatience until they were claiming it for themselves.

Moments later, the huge and menacing cowboy's shaft gave a little throb. It turned out that it was just the precursor for what was going to happen. It was now throbbing and shaking inside of me like a trapped beast, shooting out rope after rope of come.

It took it longer than I thought it was going to. When I was already feeling like he was suffocating me and I felt like I was going to pass out, he showed me he had something else planned.

Or rather, in this case, it was someone else. The other cowboy. Walter. It turned out that they resolved their differences and were now ready to claim me as their own.

Otis pulled out with a plop and my lips still felt wide and a little floppy. I heard him stepping back as his friend took over, settling his hand on the back of my head and shoving it down. He almost broke my neck!

"You're mine now, princess," he growled, making me remember that I was still a virgin. I was going to be so until the end of this, when they were both done with me and I wasn't the same person from before. I couldn't wait until I was tasting his come and finding out if it had a different flavor than his colleague's.

His balls slapping against my chin, he kept on ravaging my mouth and ramming his dick in and out of it for what felt like hours. A moment later, his cock gave a little shake. I knew that it was the precursor for what was going to happen, just like the first time.

He was going to feed me with his delicious, warm and thick milk, and I couldn't wait another second.

Thankfully, I didn't have to. One moment his balls were tensing up, and the next he was rewarding me with his warm flow.

It was thick and wasn't going down my throat as fast as I'd like, which had its upside. It meant that I could taste it for a little while longer.

He pulled out with a plopping sound and I knew that it was over. Huffing, I could tell it was going to be difficult to wait until I was their hucow. The guy who was trying to hit on me had no more chances. Not that I was even going to keep in touch with him or anything like that, though.

Actually, I was already looking forward to the next stage of my life.

CHAPTER 4

Crawling over the grass and munching on a handful of it, I jumped when a slap connected with my ass. It was one of the cowboys who was right behind me and he had a dirty smile on his face.

He wrapped his arm around me and pulled me up, forcing me against his body. I could feel how hard his muscles were and that they were pressing against my oversized boobs. Milk was seeping out of my nipples, pooling on his chest.

"You are delicious. Took you more time than I thought it was going to become who you are now, but I can see that it was worth the wait."

He raked me over with his eyes, moving his hand down my spine and then cupping my right asscheek, giving it a little squeeze. I moaned, closing my eyes as he started to peck my neck with his lips.

They were strong and wet pecks that turned me on more than I already was, imagining what it would be like if he started to milk me with his mouth. I knew that they were planning on milking me with a certain machine, but my mind was set on something else.

I groaned when he pushed me against nothing, making me fall over on my ass. He jumped on me, closing his body around me as he grabbed one of my boobs. Walter locked his eyes with me and then growled, "This here – this is all mine."

I didn't think he meant that, though. He was buddy-buddy with Otis now, right? They were okay with sharing me, weren't they? I asked myself, soon realizing that the question didn't matter right now. He pulled my boob up, enclosing his lips around the nipple. He started to tug and suck on it, drawing out milk.

All I could do was moan and groan, closing my eyes again as I felt my back rubbing against the grass. Moments later, all I could feel was his cock and balls grinding against my pussy, and I knew that just one thought was in his mind – that of breeding me.

He suckled on my nipple for what felt like hours, eventually pulling his head back with a plopping sound. I could see my milk on his lips and tongue.

"That was delicious and to think that I still have even more of it waiting for me..."

The cowboy was talking about my other boob, which was still heavy and aching to be milked. He put two of his fingers on the nipple and then pinched it, making me moan and groan as I wrapped my legs around his back.

I pulled him tightly against me as I said over and over how much I wanted him inside of me. And most of all, I wanted him to impregnate me with his babies.

It wasn't long until he was smiling devilishly again before moving his head down, wrapping his lips around my other nipple. I felt the force with which he was applying on it as he started to suck out all of my milk. It was shooting out in long ropes.

It was like his body was growing stronger as he chugged down as much of my milk as he could. His dick was so hard and it was such a pity that he wasn't taking it out anytime soon. After all, given that his eyes were closed and he was just sucking on my nipple nice and slow, I could tell he was taking his time.

With my eyes closed, I couldn't see what was happening before it was too late. When I snapped my eyelids open again, I realized that the other cowboy was right here with us on the grassy field. He yanked Walter away from me, jumping on him a moment later with the speed of a thunderbolt.

Pulling his hand up and closing it, I knew what was going to happen and I was going to stop it before it was too late. After all, as a virgin woman, the only thing I was worried about was losing my virginity. There was just one way to do it, and it was by having both of these cowboys fucking me until I was not the current person I was.

I leaped as I grabbed his shoulder and pulled him toward me. He snapped his head to glance at me, snarling as he showed me he wasn't happy about what I was doing. I never thought I was going to see Otis so angry again – and especially not against me.

I fell on my ass again and tried to scoot away from him, only to realize it wasn't going to be needed. Walter stood up, put a hand on his friend's shoulder, and said, "Melissa is right. There is no point in fighting over her. We all know what she wants and we should give it to her."

He licked his lips as if to tell me it was finally going to happen. They were going to breed me with their sperm, and it was going to be the most delicious thing that ever happened in my life. I took a deep breath in, readied myself for that, and then got back on my knees and hands on the grassy field because now it was my natural position.

They both wrapped their arms around me as they took me to the barn, where they were going to do it right in front of the other hucows.

And the thought that I was going to show it to them was turning me on more than I already was. Milk was still coming out of my nipples and my leak between my legs was more abundant now than it had ever been.

I couldn't wait until Otis and Walter were fucking my pussy until the sun was setting behind the farm.

CHAPTER 5

I groaned as Otis pushed me up against the wall, his hands groping my asscheeks like they were his. And sure enough, they were. They branded me not too long before this and I could still feel the heat of the rod when they pressed it against my skin. It had the initials of the owners of the farmhouse.

He started to pepper my neck with powerful kisses that sent shivers down my spine.

His strong and confident hands were already doing everything they wanted with my ass, opening it wide and then forcing my pussy open. I really thought that he was going to take his time, but given the speed with which this was happening, I could tell he didn't want to do that.

Not long after, he drove his dick into my cunt as he popped my hymen. It all happened like he couldn't care less that he was taking my virginity. I was pretty sure that the thought didn't even cross his mind.

The only thing that mattered to him was that now he was inside of me, so much so that he couldn't even see his balls.

He pulled me back and I stumbled over to Otis. He was right in front of me, his hands grabbing me as he licked his lips. He was yearning for just one thing – or two of them, to be more precise. When he had them, it would be like his life changed to something different.

He shoved his head down, enclosed his lips around my nipple, and started to suckle on it, chugging down all of my milk. His hands were exploring my body, and he soon found the little nub he was seeking. My clit. He scrubbed it over and over, more often than not giving it long brushes with his heavy finger.

I groaned and something exploded inside of me, making my whole body shake with pleasure. It wasn't too long until I was finally regaining my composure and could better understand what was happening around me. Otis and Walter had switched places, and now it was Otis who was yanking me to him.

He drove his dick into my pussy and then all the way up. His pace was slow in the beginning, but he soon corrected that. Every time he thrust in, lines of my milk squirted out and flew everywhere in the barn. The other hucows mooed as they wished they were right here with me.

"You know, there's something I've always been thinking about doing," Walter mentioned before pressing a button on one of the walls, and I didn't have to wait too long to know what it did. The pens' doors opened and out of them crawled the hucows.

They surrounded the pools of my milk on the soil and started to lap them up, enjoying it far more than I thought they would. One of them approached me and started to give my clit long and controlled licks, driving me over the edge again.

I couldn't resist it, my body shaking and squirming against Otis' confident hold. He dug his fingers deeper into my skin as he continued to eat my snatch bareback. And a moment later, he was finally giving me what I'd been looking for all along.

It happened all of a sudden.

One moment he was just sliding in and out of me, and the next he was throbbing inside my tunnel. I clenched it tight around his dick and milked him for all he had. One long rope of sperm after the other, he impregnated me and I couldn't wait until I was carrying his heir – or heirs – inside my belly with a smug on my face.

Otis stayed still inside of me, only pulling out when he had his fill. I thought he was going to last a little longer, but he didn't plan on doing that. When he was out, he was out with a pop and my pussy lips felt looser than before. I didn't think they'd ever return to how they were.

I fell on all fours and when I thought I was going to be granted some minutes to recompose myself, Walter yanked me to him and rammed his dick inside my pussy without showing a hint of mercy. He was hilt-deep and eating me raw like he thought this was his last fuck.

"Jesus," he groaned into my ear, nibbling on my earlobe as he dug his fingers deeper into my skin. I squealed and mooed as a wave of pure orgasm swept through me.

The man erupted inside of me, making me feel loved, fucked, eaten up raw, and so many other things I couldn't even describe. My body rocked and I fell on my back when he pulled out.

They both turned, surrounded the other hucows, who were in turn surrounding me. I smiled even though I shouldn't be. I should be trying to breathe and recompose my energies, but it looked like they weren't going to give me the chance.

The hucows started to please me in more ways than one, some with their bellies big and heavy. I couldn't wait until I was looking just like them.

Walter and Otis fucked one of them at a time, knocking up the ones that weren't. When they were done, they took off on horseback and went to the nearest town naked. I had no idea what they were thinking, but I was still pretty sure that it involved them knocking up all other virgin women they could find.

They were going to build their hucow empire and I was glad I was a part of it.

The End

Looking for the first 5 books in the series? Download them here:

1. Cowboys' Lucky Age Gap

2. Cowboys' Naughty Age Gap

3. Cowboys' Christmas Age Gap

4. Cowboys' Medical Age Gap
5. Cowboys' Mafia Age Gap

Lastly, leave a review if you liked this book. It really helps me.

SNEAK PEEK: COWBOYS' LUCKY AGE GAP

Fertile First Time Thanksgiving Story (Hucow Milking Farm - 1)

Perhaps everything would be so much easier if that hunk of a man wasn't seated across from me. We were in the dining room, and I wasn't alone.

His colleague was also with us, picking up a glass of wine and taking a sip from it. His eyes were locked with mine and it was like he was trying to read my mind.

I wasn't trying to read his mind, but I was ogling him without making it obvious I was doing that. I had no idea if he was picking that up, but he smiled and I could see the beautifulness of his super white teeth.

I was just checking him out, wishing I could be in his arms. They looked so strong, confident, veins popping out where I could more easily see them, hair in all the right places, and his skin tanned by the light of the sun. I'd been fantasizing about him since coming here.

And it wasn't just Walter's arms that made my pussy wet, but also his face. And more specifically, his lips.

I wouldn't say that they were big, but they look just right and I knew that if I were kissing them now, I'd be tasting how sweet they were.

His face was chiseled and looked perfect. He groomed his full, thick beard every day, and it looked sharp without making him look gay.

It gave him that extra spice of manliness I always craved in a man. Looking down slightly, I also loved how his beard transitioned to his neck. I could just imagine myself lying in his bed with him and cradling my head in the crook of his neck. I was pretty sure he would love it if I did that.

But something was impeding me from doing that, and it was the fact that I was a virgin. I didn't know much about these two guys, but I knew that they craved women that had a lot more experience.

I didn't want to disappoint them or myself.

His blond hair seemed to draw my attention to him, and I couldn't control that I was ogling it too. It was short, a bit bigger at the top, and even shorter at the sides. I had no idea if he got his hair cut often, but it was always sharp. This wasn't the first time I was checking him out, after all.

His eyes were icy blue and I suddenly found myself entranced by them. His eyes showed me that behind his tough persona, he was a free-spirited and extroverted man. I didn't need that to tell me that was what he was like, but it was great having that confirmation again.

Seated beside him was his colleague. He was forking a piece of meat on his plate, and I noticed the veins popping out on his forearms. His skin was also white, but just as tanned.

He didn't have a full beard like Walter, but his stubble actually made him look sexier. I could just imagine what it would be like to be grazing my hands over his chin and jawline, feeling the roughness of his skin.

MORE HUCOW BOOKS

SERIES - FAVORITE HUCOWS

1. First Time in the Barn: A Fertile Harem Story

2. First Time in the Pen: A Fertile Harem Story

3. First Time in the Shed: A Fertile Harem Story

4. First Time in the Tractor: A Fertile Harem Story

5. First Time on the Haystack: A Fertile Harem Story

SERIES - FERTILE ONLY

1. Bumping the Teacher: A Hucow Mafia First Time Story

2. Bumping the Midwife: A Hucow Mafia First Time Story

3. Bumping the Farmhand: A Hucow Mafia First Time Story

4. Bumping the Sinner: A Hucow Mafia First Time Story

SERIES - HUCOW FOR WHITE COLLARS

1. Milked by the Lawyers: A First Time Bimbo Ménage Story

2. Milked by Doctors: A First Time Bimbo Ménage Story

3. Milked by Engineers: A First Time Bimbo Ménage Story

4. Milked by Directors: A First Time Bimbo Ménage Story

5. Milked by Managers: A First Time Bimbo Ménage Story

And you can also get these fertile hucow mega bundles:

Creaming the Bimbo: A Fertile Hucow MEGA Collection

Milked by Cowboys: A Hucow Milking MEGA Bundle

Milked for Christmas: 15 First Time Hucow Stories

Fertile Leakers: 10 Milking Stories

Milked, Shared and Used: 16 Stories of Milking Ladies

ABOUT THE AUTHOR

Leandra's Camilli's obsession? Writing dirty, steamy stories that will make you drool. She loves her Alpha males, hucows, sissies, and futas. If you're looking for that kind of book, you've found the right author page.

With a cup of coffee on her table and warm socks on, she writes almost every day. Leandra Camilli's been present in several top 100 categories in the store, and she always finishes her stories.

Facebook: https://www.facebook.com/lcerotic
Mailing list: https://mailchi.mp/ef21b6cb3a67/leandra_camilli

www.ingramcontent.com/pod-product-compliance
Lightning Source LLC
Chambersburg PA
CBHW071507150726
48000CB00006B/2734